JOURNEY TO CRYSTAL LAKE

Young Adult Romance

Part One

LIA LUCAS

Ardent Artist Books

Journey to Crystal Lake - Part One
Copyright © 2024 by Lia Lucas
All rights reserved.

Book Cover and formatting provided by Trisha Fuentes
https://bit.ly/m/trishafuentes

ISBN: 979-8-3302-6153-6 (Paperback)

Published by
Ardent Artist Books
www.ardentartistbooks.com

About Ardent Artist Books

Ardent Artist Books was established in 2008.

We publish modern and historical romances once a month!

For a complete list of our published books and books in development, please visit our website at:

https://ardentartistbooks.com/free-downloads

FREE DOWNLOAD
Updated Monthly!

Follow us on YouTube to see what new stories are on the horizon!

https://www.youtube.com/theardentartist

Like, Subscribe & Comment

LET'S CONNECT!

Fuel your love of fiction with exclusive content and captivating insights from Ardent Artist Books. Whether you crave the thrill of modern narratives or the timeless elegance of historical fiction, our newsletter delivers a curated selection straight to your inbox.

Plus, as a welcome gift, receive a FREE downloadable eBook:

"The Family Fix"

https://mailchi.mp/567874a61a56/aab-landing-page

Chapter One

SEQUOIA GROVE HIGH

Madison "Maddie" Sullivan closed her eyes, soaking in the warmth of the sun on her face. The gentle caress of grass tickled her legs as she sat cross-legged on the school lawn, her best friend Brooke Jackson, beside her. The distant chatter of their classmates faded into background noise as they delved into their conversation.

"So, what's the plan for winter break?" Brooke asked, her hazel eyes sparkling with curiosity.

Maddie's heart quickened with anticipation. "The annual Sullivan camping *extravaganza*," she replied, a grin spreading across her face. "I can't wait to get back to Crystal Lake."

"Ooh, tell me more!" Brooke leaned in, her curls bouncing with enthusiasm.

Maddie's mind drifted to the campsite, its image as clear as a photograph in her mind. "Picture this: towering pines stretching towards the sky, their branches like outstretched arms welcoming us home. The lake, so still it's like a mirror reflecting the clouds." She inhaled deeply, almost able to smell the crisp mountain air. "And the best part? No cell service. Just us and nature."

Brooke wrinkled her nose. "No cell service? How will you survive?"

Maddie laughed, the sound light and carefree. "That's the beauty of it, Brookie. No distractions, no stress. Just family, campfires, and the great outdoors."

As she spoke, Maddie's fingers absently traced patterns in the grass. She thought about the upcoming trip, a mix of excitement and nostalgia washing over her. These camping trips had been a constant in her life, a touchstone she could always rely on. In a world of constant change, they were her anchor.

"You really love it out there, don't you?" Brooke observed, her voice soft with understanding.

Maddie nodded, her eyes distant. "It's where I feel most like myself," she admitted. "Like I can breathe easier, think clearer. Does that sound crazy?"

"Not at all," Brooke assured her, reaching out to squeeze Maddie's hand. "It sounds perfect."

Maddie smiled, grateful for her friend's support. She glanced around the bustling school grounds, a stark contrast to the serenity of Crystal Lake. For a moment, she felt a pang of longing for the simplicity of camp life. "Dad's promised to teach us how to read the stars," she said, her voice filled with excitement. "And Mom wants to try some new campfire recipes. Oh, and I'm determined to finally conquer that hiking trail that kicked my butt last year."

As she spoke, Maddie's hands moved animatedly, painting pictures in the air. She could almost feel the cool mountain air on her skin, hear the crackle of the campfire, taste the s'mores melting on her tongue.

"It sounds amazing, Mad," Brooke said, her smile genuine. "I wish I could bottle up some of that excitement for my own break."

Maddie paused, suddenly aware of how much she'd been gushing. "Sorry, I didn't mean to go on and on," she said, feeling a twinge of guilt. "What about *you*? Any plans?"

As Brooke opened her mouth to respond, the bell rang, signaling the end of lunch. Maddie sighed, reluctantly pulled back to reality. The thought of returning to classes after such a pleasant daydream felt like a bucket of cold water.

"To be continued?" she suggested, gathering her things.

Brooke nodded, springing to her feet with her usual energy. "Definitely. And Mad? Thanks for letting me live vicariously through your camping adventures."

Maddie smiled, warmth blooming in her chest. As they headed back into the school building, she held onto the lingering feeling of excitement. Winter break couldn't come soon enough.

BROOKE'S hazel eyes lit up, her curly hair bouncing as she nodded enthusiastically. "Oh my gosh, Mad, I can't wait to tell you about *my* plans!" She clasped her hands together, her voice bubbling with excitement. "I'm visiting Nana and Pop-Pop for the whole break!"

Maddie couldn't help but smile at her friend's infectious joy. "That's awesome, Brooke. You're super close with them, right?"

"The closest!" Brooke exclaimed, her words tumbling out in a rush. "I haven't seen my grandparents in over a year, and Nana's already planning all these amazing baking sessions. She promised to teach me her secret Snickerdoodle recipe this time." She paused, a mischievous glint in her eye. "And Pop-Pop? He's been hinting at some big surprise. I'm dying to know what it is!"

As Brooke continued to chatter about her grandparents' cozy house and the traditions they shared, Maddie found her attention suddenly diverted. A group of boys had emerged from the school building, their laughter carrying across the lawn. At their center was Dexter "Dex" Matthews, his blonde hair catching the sunlight as he joked with his friends.

Maddie's heart skipped a beat. She tried to focus on Brooke's words, but her eyes kept darting back to Dex. His easy smile, the way he ran his hand through his hair – it was infuriatingly distracting.

"...and then we always—Maddie? Are you even listening?" Brooke's voice snapped her back to reality.

"Sorry, I just..." Maddie trailed off, her cheeks warming. She glanced meaningfully in Dex's direction.

Brooke followed her gaze, understanding dawning on her face. "Oh," she said, her voice dropping to a whisper. "I see what's caught your attention."

Maddie bit her lip, torn between embarrassment and the urge to keep watching Dex. "I didn't mean to zone out on you," she murmured. "It's just... you know."

Brooke nudged her playfully. "Trust me, I get it. He's hard to ignore."

As they both stole glances at Dex and his friends, Maddie felt a mix of excitement and nervousness flutter in her stomach. She wondered, not for the first time, what it would be like to be part of that effortlessly cool group.

Maddie sighed, twisting a blade of hair between her fingers. "It's not fair," she murmured, her eyes still fixed on Dex. "How can someone be that... perfect?"

Brooke nodded, her usual bubbly energy subdued. "I know, right? It's like he walked out of a teen movie or something."

"Yeah," Maddie agreed, her voice tinged with longing. "But we're definitely not the leading ladies in *that* movie."

A burst of laughter from Dex's group made both girls

jump. Maddie's heart raced as Dex's blue eyes swept across the lawn, briefly meeting hers before moving on.

"Did you see that?" Brooke whispered excitedly. "He looked over here!"

Maddie shook her head, trying to quell the hope rising in her chest. "Come on, Brookie. Guys like Dex don't notice girls like us. We're practically invisible."

"Maybe," Brooke conceded, but her tone was lighter. "But a girl can dream, right?"

Maddie allowed herself a small smile, glancing once more at Dex. "Yeah," she said softly. "I guess we can always dream."

Maddie shook her head, forcibly tearing her gaze away from Dex and his friends. She turned to Brooke, her hazel eyes brightening with a different kind of excitement. "Anyway, enough about impossible crushes. Tell me more about your grandparents' place. I bet it's going to be amazing! They live by the beach, right?"

Brooke's face lit up, her curls bouncing as she nodded eagerly. "Oh my gosh, Maddie, you have no idea! Nana's already promised to teach me how to surf. Can you believe it?"

Maddie grinned, picturing Brooke covered in sand, her body gliding across the ocean waves. "That's awesome, Brookie. Your Nana is legendary."

"I know, right?" Brooke giggled, then leaned in conspiratorially. "But what about you? Crystal Lake must be gorgeous in winter. I'm so jealous you get to spend your break surrounded by all that nature."

"And I'm so jealous of you escaping the winter to bask in the sun's glow!" Maddie said, hugging her books close to her chest.

"Look at us—I'm going to the beach, while you're going camping!"

Maddie's heart swelled with anticipation. She could almost smell the crisp pine air, feel the crunch of snow beneath her boots. "It's like stepping into another world," she said softly. "Everything's so quiet and still, except for the occasional crack of ice on the lake."

"Sounds magical," Brooke sighed. "Way more exciting than learning to surf."

Maddie shook her head, reaching out to squeeze her friend's hand. "Hey, don't sell yourself short. Family time is just as magical. Besides," she added with a wry smile, "you won't have to worry about bears stealing your food."

Brooke's laughter at Maddie's bear comment was cut short by a sudden commotion. Maddie's heart skipped a beat as she caught sight of Dex Matthews and his friends sauntering across the grass, their carefree laughter drifting on the breeze.

Maddie's breath hitched. Dex's tousled blonde hair caught the sunlight, and even from a distance, she could see the mischievous glint in his deep blue eyes. She tried to look away, but her gaze was magnetically drawn to his athletic frame and easy grace.

"There he is again," Brooke whispered, her voice barely audible.

Maddie nodded, not trusting her voice. She could feel a blush creeping up her neck, and she silently cursed her fair complexion. *Why did Dex have to look so effortlessly handsome all the time?*

As if sensing their attention, Dex glanced their way. For a split second, his eyes met Maddie's, and she felt a jolt of electricity course through her. She quickly looked down, pretending to be fascinated by the row of lockers.

When she dared to look up again, Dex and his friends had passed by, their laughter fading into the distance. Maddie's eyes met Brooke's, and in that silent exchange, she saw her own feelings mirrored in her best friend's face

— a mixture of longing, embarrassment, and the unspoken acknowledgment of their shared crush.

Maddie's mind raced. *Did Dex notice them? Did he think they were staring?* She wanted to say something, anything, to break the tension, but the words stuck in her throat.

Maddie cleared her throat, desperate to dispel the awkward silence. "So, um... that happened," she said, her voice a mix of amusement and embarrassment.

Brooke giggled, her bubbly personality resurfacing. "Oh my gosh, Maddie! Did you see how his hair was all perfectly messy? How does he even do that?"

"Probably takes him hours," Maddie quipped, rolling her eyes playfully. "I bet he has a special 'tousle spray' or something."

"Tousle spray!" Brooke burst into laughter, her curls bouncing. "Can you imagine? 'Dex Matthews' Patented Heartthrob Hair Mist — Guaranteed to Make Girls Swoon!'"

Maddie snorted, grateful for the tension-breaking humor. "You're ridiculous."

"Says the girl who practically drooled when he walked by," Brooke teased, nudging Maddie's shoulder.

Maddie felt her cheeks flush again. "I didn't drool! I was just... appreciating the scenery."

"Uh-huh, sure," Brooke winked. "The Dex-shaped scenery."

They dissolved into giggles, the shared moment of crushing and subsequent teasing solidifying their friendship. As their laughter subsided, Maddie found her thoughts drifting back to their earlier conversation.

"Hey," she said, her tone growing more serious. "I know we'll be apart for break, but promise we'll text every day? I want to hear all about your surfing lessons."

Brooke's eyes lit up. "Only if you promise to send me pictures of the stars over Crystal Lake. I bet they're amazing out there."

Maddie nodded, a wave of excitement washing over her at the thought of the upcoming camping trip. "It's a deal. Who knows? Maybe this will be the year I finally learn to fish without tangling the line."

"And maybe I'll finally beat Pop-Pop at chess," Brooke added with a grin.

As the bell signaling the end of lunch rang out across the grounds of Sequoia Grove High School, Maddie felt a bittersweet mix of emotions. She was eager for the adventures that lay ahead, but a small part of her wished she could freeze this moment with her best friend, their shared secrets and laughter a buffer against the uncertainties of the future.

Chapter Two

JOURNEY TO CRYSTAL LAKE

Maddie's room was an island in a sea of camping gear. Thermal sweaters and thick socks lay in neat stacks waiting for her touch, like loyal companions eager for the next journey. With each piece of clothing she folded, Maddie's heart danced a little faster. The mountains called to her, whispering promises of pine-scented air and skies so wide they swallowed your troubles whole.

She tucked her clothes into the backpack with precision, as if every fold sealed in a memory yet to be made. The fabric rustled softly, a prelude to the symphony of wilderness sounds that would soon surround her at Crystal Lake Camp Ground. A smile played on her lips, her thoughts drifting to the trails she'd conquer, the campfire stories yet to echo in the night.

Her gaze landed on the sturdy hiking boots lined up by the door—silent sentinels of past and future treks. She reached for them, her fingers grazing the rough leather that had protected her feet through seasons of adventure. Each scuff and scratch told a story of resilience, much like the calluses on her own palms—a testament to the miles she'd walked and the challenges she'd faced.

Sitting cross-legged on the floor, Maddie cradled one boot between her knees, threading the laces with deliberate care. Every tug tightened the bond between her and the path ahead, the sharp zipping sound of the laces like a countdown to the moment she'd step onto the familiar trail. She relished the snug embrace of the boots as they molded to her feet—a grounding force ready to carry her across streams and up the rugged spine of the mountains.

With each lace secured, Maddie rose to her feet, her stance firm and purposeful. These boots were more than mere footwear; they were a promise of the self-discovery that awaited her with each crest and valley she'd navigate. They were freedom, etched in leather and threaded with hope, a perfect fit not just for her feet, but for her wandering spirit, eager to explore the vast canvas of nature's masterpiece.

With a determined stride, Maddie crossed her room, her boots thudding against the hardwood floor. She came to a halt in front of her full-length mirror, taking a moment to admire the worn leather of her favorite boots before looking up to examine her appearance. Her chestnut hair cascaded down her back in gentle waves, longer than usual but still falling just at her waist. She absentmindedly twirled a lock of hair around her finger, enjoying the weight and warmth of it. Wisps of hair framed her face, giving her an effortless bohemian look.

Her gaze moved to her reflection's eyes - green-brown and flecked with gold. They were naturally striking, but she often felt like they were overshadowed by Brooke Jackson's bright blue eyes that always seemed to draw attention. She shrugged off the thought, reminding herself that beauty was subjective.

Mascara was not a regular part of Maddie's makeup routine, but occasionally she would add some for a subtle enhancement. However, her mother had always told her that she didn't need it - her dark lashes were naturally defined and long enough to flutter against her cheekbones. As she studied herself in the mirror, Maddie couldn't deny that she was naturally pretty. But as the constant companion to someone as stunning as Brooke Jackson, it was easy to feel overlooked.

Nonetheless, Maddie squared her shoulders and left the room with confidence, ready to take on the day.

Maddie descended the stairs, the weight of her packed backpack a comforting anchor against her shoulders. She stepped into the kitchen, where the aroma of simmering stew mingled with the homely scent of freshly baked bread. At the stove, her mother, Laura stirred a pot, her movements fluid and practiced.

"Mom, I can't believe we're finally going," Maddie said, her voice bubbling over with eagerness. "I feel like this trip is going to be amazing."

Laura glanced over her shoulder, her green eyes crinkling at the corners as she smiled. "I'm sure it will be, sweetheart. Just remember to be careful and make the most of every moment." Her words were a gentle breeze, encouraging yet cautious.

"I will, Mom." Maddie's response was a whisper of leaves against the windowpane—a quiet promise to cherish the beauty and lessons the wilderness offered.

The kitchen door swung open, revealing her father, John in his utilitarian outdoor attire, a symphony of zippers and Velcro. His presence seemed to fill the room, a steadfast oak in their family grove.

"Ready to load up the car?" he asked, his voice the rumble of distant thunder.

"Absolutely!" Maddie replied, her spirit soaring like an eagle at the prospect of contributing. Together, they ventured into the garage, where camping gear lay stacked in orderly piles—each item a note in the melody of their preparation.

John hoisted a cooler, his muscles flexing beneath his jacket, while Maddie grabbed the tent. The canvas and poles were a dragon she was determined to tame. As she lifted the bundle, a sense of accomplishment swelled within her chest. She was the keeper of their shelter, a role she embraced with pride.

"Thanks, Madison," John said, a nod of approval lighting up his eyes. His simple acknowledgment was a badge of honor pinned to Maddie's heart, affirming her place in this annual ritual. Together, father and daughter moved in harmony, a dance of readiness for the journey ahead.

Maddie balanced the weight of the sleeping bags in her arms, the fabric rustling like whispers of anticipation as she maneuvered them into the trunk of the car. Her breath misted in the crisp morning air, the day already hinting at the adventures to come. She was a ship ready to set sail, her cargo packed tight and secure.

The buzz of her phone broke the rhythm of her tasks, a beacon of modern life amidst the timeless ritual of preparation. Maddie set the sleeping bags down with care, freeing her hands to retrieve the device from her jacket pocket. It was Brooke, her words lighting up the screen with that familiar effervescent energy.

> Can't believe you're heading off again! 🐨 Send me tons of pics, okay?! 🌲

Each emoji is a sprinkle of Brooke's sparkling personality.

Maddie's thumbs danced over the keyboard, a smile tugging at the corners of her mouth.

> Will do! Can't wait to tell you all about it when I get back. ⛺

"Here, take this with you." The voice was soft, but carried the warmth of a hearth fire. Laura stood in the doorway, a silver thermos cradled in her hands like a precious artifact. It was an old, dented thing, the surface etched with memories of campfires past.

"Thanks, Mom," Maddie said as she took the thermos, the metal cool against her skin. She twisted the cap open just enough to let the rich scent of cocoa escape. It mingled with the pine-scented breeze, a blend of home and wilderness that spoke directly to her soul.

"Be sure to share it with your dad," Laura added, her green eyes twinkling with unspoken stories. "He'll need the warmth after setting up camp."

Maddie nodded, her grip on the thermos firm. This wasn't just a drink; it was a tradition steeped in love, a reminder that no matter how far she roamed, the heart of her family would always be close by.

"Will do," she assured, her voice carrying the promise of shared moments under the vast mountain sky. She tucked the thermos into her backpack, its presence a steady pulse against her back—a reassurance of the bonds that tethered her to this world.

As she zipped her pack closed, the finality of the gesture marked the end of one chapter and the beginning of another. All around her, the Sullivan family moved with purpose, each step a note in the symphony of their departure. Maddie's heart thrummed with the rhythm of the mountains calling, her spirit alight with the flames of adventure yet to come.

MADDIE CLIMBED INTO THE BACKSEAT, her backpack a faithful companion at her side. The Sullivan's family sedan hummed to life, its engine a soft purr that melded with the quiet anticipation hanging in the air.

Outside the window, Sequoia Grove's cozy storefronts and leaf-strewn sidewalks receded, replaced by the open road stretching out like a ribbon toward distant peaks.

"Remember the year the raccoons stole our marshmallows?" Maddie's voice broke the silence, a smile playing on her lips as she glanced at her parents in the front seats.

Her mother laughed, the sound warm and full. "How could I forget? Your father turned into quite the detective trying to track them down."

"Ah, but the real mystery was how they unzipped the tent," her dad chimed in, his eyes meeting Maddie's in the rearview mirror. "Those critters are more cunning than they look."

Laughter bubbled up from Maddie's throat, the memory vivid as if painted across the sky. Trees blurred past the car, their branches reaching for each other like old friends sharing secrets. The Sullivan family wove tales of past adventures into the fabric of the journey, each word a stitch binding them closer.

"Or the time we hiked to Crystal Lake, and you caught that giant trout," Maddie said, her eyes sparkling with the recollection of triumph against the silvery flash of fish.

"Only to throw it back," her mom added with a gentle smile. "You've always had a soft heart for living things, Madison."

"True," Maddie admitted, her gaze drifting to the mountains ahead. They rose like sentinels guarding the horizon, their snow-capped peaks a testament to nature's enduring strength—a reflection of the resilience Maddie felt within herself.

Maddie's dad gazed at her through the rear-view mirror, his eyes reflecting a mixture of concern and excitement. "What does the weather app say for Crystal Lake, Mads?" he asked.

Maddie met his gaze with a determined look. She quickly reached for her phone and tapped on the weather app, scrolling through the county to find Crystal Lake. "Let me take a look," she replied confidently.

As she scrolled through the forecast, she felt a chill run down her spine. "It says...a crisp and sunny day in the high 50s," she announced, trying to suppress her growing anxiety.

Her dad turned to her mom in the passenger seat. "Good thing I packed those extra blankets," he said with a slight smile.

Maddie continued scrolling through the rest of the forecast, her brow furrowing in confusion. "It also says 'potential low clouds'. What does that mean?" she asked, turning to her parents for answers.

Her mom twisted around in her seat to face them in the back. "Snow," she stated matter-of-factly. "But we won't worry about it. I think I read somewhere that the storm won't hit Crystal Lake."

Maddie took a deep breath, trying to push away her fears as they drove towards their destination. She could only hope that her mother was right and that their trip wouldn't be ruined by unexpected snowfall.

The road wound its way through the foothills, each turn revealing new vistas that spoke of the untamed beauty waiting to embrace them. Conversation flowed effortlessly, the Sullivan's shared history a tapestry rich with laughter and learning, the threads of which Maddie clung to as the familiar faded behind them.

"Can't wait to make new memories," Maddie mused aloud, her words tinged with excitement and the faintest hint of longing—for experiences yet unknown, paths yet untrodden.

"Every trip is a blank page," her dad said, glancing at her

again with that knowing look that seemed to peer right into her soul. "And we get to write the story together."

As the car climbed higher, the air grew crisper, the scent of pine seeping in through the cracks in the windows. Maddie drew a deep breath, letting the coolness fill her lungs, tasting the promise of tomorrow's adventures on her tongue.

"Here's to the next chapter," she whispered, her voice barely audible over the rush of wind. It was a vow to the mountains, to the wild, and to the journey of self-discovery that awaited her just around the bend.

Chapter Three

SETTING UP CAMP

The Sullivan family car rolled to a gentle halt, the gravel beneath its tires crackling like a quiet round of applause. Crystal Lake Camp Ground welcomed them, an oasis amidst the grandeur of the pines that soared skyward. Maddie's heart skipped as she swung open the door, her sneakers crunching on the forest's carpet. The scent of pine enveloped her, rich and pure, the very essence of freedom she yearned for every year.

"Here we are," she breathed out, more to herself than anyone else, her gaze tracing the outlines of nature's skyscrapers.

"Looks like the perfect spot," her mother agreed, peering over her shoulder at the expanse of greenery. They all knew the routine—a symphony of unpacking and setting up camp, a rhythm that Maddie fell into with ease.

She reached for the tent bag, its weight familiar in her hands. With a fluid motion born from years of practice, the tent unfurled, fabric whispering secrets of nights under the stars. Her father handed her the stakes, his nod an unspoken communication they both understood. Maddie's fingers worked methodically, pushing each metal spike into the forgiving earth. The stakes sank home, anchoring their temporary abode in the world of wilderness—a sentinel against the night.

"Nice job, Madison," her dad said with a hint of pride. His words were simple but held the weight of his expectations, ones Maddie aimed to meet—one stake, one challenge at a time.

"Thanks, Dad." She straightened, surveying the tent with a critical eye. It stood strong and proud, a canvas castle for their upcoming nightly retreats. She could almost hear the soft flutter of conversation within its walls, the whispers of the mountain wind joining in as if eager to share its own tales.

"Can't wait to cozy up in there," Maddie mused, a wistful smile playing on her lips. Her thoughts danced with visions of the evenings ahead: the warmth of shared blankets, the soft glow of flashlights casting shadows on the tent walls, the hushed thrill of feeling utterly small beneath the vastness of the heavens.

"Neither can we," her mom replied, bringing Maddie back to the crisp air and fading light. There was much to do before darkness embraced the campsite, yet this moment—this snapshot of accomplishment—Maddie tucked away in her heart, a keepsake for colder days.

Her parents busied themselves with the next task, but Maddie lingered a second longer, her eyes following the ascent of a lone bird into the evening sky. Adventure called to her from the treetops whispered along the breeze, and nestled in the corners of her dreams. Here, among these ancient sentinels, she felt the pull of something greater—a promise of self-discovery wrapped in the embrace of the wild.

"Come on, Maddie," her dad beckoned, "let's get the firewood before it gets too dark."

"Coming!" With one last glance at their fabric fortress, Maddie stepped away, ready to forge memories in the flickering light of the campfire, under the watchful gaze of the stars.

· · ·

MADDIE STOOD BACK, hands on hips, surveying the campsite. Tent pitched and gear stowed, the space had transformed from a patch of earth to their cozy home base. She let out a slow exhale, her breath visible in the chilled air, mingling with the scent of pine and wild freedom. The mountains around her stood as silent guardians, their peaks brushing against the fabric of the sky. It was here, amidst the whisper of leaves and the soft crunch of needles underfoot, that Maddie felt an anchor drop deep into her soul, rooting her to this moment, to this fragment of untamed world.

She closed her eyes, letting the mountain's quiet heartbeat sync with her own. A smile curved her lips as peace draped over her shoulders like a well-worn jacket, comforting and familiar. This was her haven, the place where the clamor of high school hallways and the weight of expectations dissolved into the crisp air. Here, she was free to be Madison Sullivan, the girl who craved adventure more than applause, whose spirit thrived in the boundless embrace of nature.

The buzz of her phone snapped her from reverie. With reluctant fingers, she pulled it from her pocket, already anticipating Brooke's enthusiastic words on the screen, a digital echo of her vivacious presence.

"Guess who's queen of the campsite?"

She typed, attaching a snapshot of their setup, the tent nestled like a promise between the pines. Maddie hit send, a grin tugging at her cheeks, ready for the volley of exclamation points and heart emojis sure to come.

But the screen blinked and faded to black before her message could take flight. Maddie tapped the power button, her frown deepening when the device remained lifeless. The realization dawned, a slow, sinking feeling—the notorious dead zone of Crystal Lake Camp Ground had claimed another victim. She shook her head with a resigned chuckle; no matter how many times they came here, some part of her always forgot about the lackluster cell service.

Pocketing the useless phone, Maddie cast a glance toward the lake, its surface reflecting the dusk-tinted sky. She'd have to store up stories in her mind, crafting them into treasures to share with Brookie upon return. For now, the digital silence offered a gift—a chance to listen to the deeper conversations of the forest, the tales woven by wind and wildlife, beckoning her to explore and discover.

"Ready to conquer the trails tomorrow?" her mother called, her voice carrying the shared anticipation of the adventures ahead.

"Absolutely," Maddie responded, her spirits undimmed by the temporary disconnection. After all, this was just the beginning, and the mountains held secrets only the patient and present could unearth. She turned her gaze upward, where the first stars began to wink into existence, mapping out the night's endless possibilities. Tomorrow awaited, ripe with the promise of self-discovery and the allure of paths untrodden.

ARMS LADEN with tinder and kindling, Maddie danced between the shadows cast by the setting sun, her steps light on the carpet of pine needles. The forest was alive with the golden hour's glow, each beam of light a spotlight for the evening's final act. Her parents' laughter mingled with the rustle of leaves, a soundtrack to their collective effort.

"Watch your step, Madison," her dad cautioned as she skirted a protruding root, his protective gaze following her every move.

"Got it, Dad," she replied with a grin, balancing her load of firewood like a seasoned trailblazer. They made their way back to the campsite, the heart of their temporary home in the wilderness.

Flames soon licked hungrily at the evening air, crackling into life as twilight embraced the campgrounds. Maddie nestled into a canvas chair, the fire's warmth caressing her cheeks. She wrapped her fingers around the thermos her mother had prepared, the metal cool against her skin. With a gentle twist, she poured the steaming cocoa into the waiting cup, its rich aroma a familiar embrace.

She brought the cup to her lips, the liquid sweetness a balm to the chill that crept in with the night. There was something sacred about this ritual, a thread woven through the tapestry of family tradition. As she savored each sip, gratitude swelled within her—a silent thank you for moments like these, simple yet profound.

Her mother's voice broke through the quiet, "It's nice, isn't it? Just us, the stars, and the promise of tomorrow."

"Perfect," Maddie agreed, the word a soft exhalation of contentment. Here, surrounded by nature's grandeur and the people she loved most, Maddie felt an anchor drop within her, holding her steady in the vast sea of the world's uncertainties.

The fire popped, a spark flying up to join the first stars in their nightly vigil. Watching the embers rise and fade, Maddie felt the day's adventures ebb away, leaving behind a canvas of night painted with possibilities.

Maddie tilted her head back, the chair cradling her as she gazed up at the celestial canvas unfurling above. Diamonds seemed to scatter across the black velvet sky, each star a beacon of adventure calling to her wanderer's heart. The constellations whispered tales of ancient travelers and lovers, stories that Maddie felt stitched into the fabric of her own dreams.

A cool breeze brushed past, stirring the pines that stood like silent guardians around the campsite. She breathed in deeply, the scent of pine resin mingling with campfire smoke, a fragrance that spoke of wild places untouched by time's relentless march.

"Look, Madison," her father said, pointing upwards. "The Big Dipper."

She followed his finger to the cluster of stars, nodding in recognition. It was a sight familiar from countless nights spent in these mountains, yet it never failed to stir something deep within her—perhaps the same primal connection our ancestors felt when they too looked up and sought guidance from those distant suns.

"Tomorrow we'll hike to the ridge," her mother chimed in, her voice soft yet edged with excitement. "Remember the view from up there?"

How could she forget? The world opened up on that ridge, a panorama of peaks and valleys stretching to eternity. Anticipation fluttered in Maddie's chest, her mind racing ahead to the rugged trails that awaited their footsteps.

"Can't wait," Maddie murmured, her words barely more than a breath lost to the night.

Eventually, the conversation dwindled, leaving only the crackling of the fire and the rustle of nocturnal creatures in the underbrush. Her parents retired to the tent, their quiet goodnights a tender lullaby that drifted through the air.

Alone with her thoughts, Maddie let her eyes roam the vastness above once more. A shooting star streaked across the sky, a fleeting brushstroke of light that sparked a silent wish in her heart—a wish for courage, for strength, and perhaps for a chance to uncover the hidden depths of her own spirit.

She unzipped her sleeping bag, the nylon whispering as she slipped inside. The ground was firm beneath her, but her air mattress squished and melded to her form.

Her eyelids grew heavy, the day's excitement melting into a serene tiredness that pulled her toward sleep. With one last look at the sky through her tent's skylight, she surrendered to slumber's gentle call.

Chapter Four

SEQUOIA GROVE HIGH

The afternoon sun cast long shadows across the Sequoia Grove High football field where Dexter "Dex" Matthews, with a pigskin cradled in his arm, darted through an obstacle course of teammates. His cleats dug into the grass, each pivot and fake sending tufts flying. Muscles tensed and released as he launched the football in a perfect spiral to a receiver downfield. Cheers erupted from the sidelines, affirming Dex's place as the junior varsity quarterback, the guy who could make plays happen when they counted most.

"Nice throw, Matthews!" one of his teammates called out, thumping him on the back with a camaraderie that only shared sweat and ambition could forge.

"Thanks, but it's all in the wrist," Dex said, flashing a grin that lit up his deep blue eyes. The breeze caught his tousled blonde hair, and for a moment, he looked like something out of a movie – the quintessential high school hero, easygoing and effortlessly charming.

"Sure, and I suppose those ballet lessons are paying off too, huh?" teased another teammate, dodging as Dex playfully swung his towel at him.

"Absolutely," Dex quipped, his tone light, "grace of a swan, remember?"

Laughter mingled with the clatter of helmets and pads as the practice wound down. Dex moved among his friends, offering a joke here, a pat on the shoulder there—each gesture reinforcing bonds that went beyond the game. It was clear that Dex thrived in these moments, his carefree spirit infectious, drawing others into his orbit of optimism.

"Hey, you coming to the bonfire Friday night?" one of the receivers asked, slinging an arm around Dex's shoulders.

"Wouldn't miss it," Dex replied, his smile unwavering. "You know me, any excuse to spin a good ghost story under the stars."

"Or maybe just to see Brooke Jackson?" another teammate chimed in with a cheeky nudge. A subtle shift passed over Dex's expression, a fleeting cloud that suggested depths not often displayed on the field. But it vanished as quickly as it came, replaced by his usual confident ease.

"Who knows what the night will bring?" Dex countered, deflecting with charm. It was his way of keeping things light, even when his heart harbored secrets heavier than the football he so expertly handled.

As the laughter faded and the players dispersed, Dex lingered on the field, breathing in the crisp air tinged with the scent of freshly cut grass. He gazed at the goalposts standing tall against the sky, their presence a reminder of challenges met and those still waiting on the horizon. For now, though, it was enough to live in the moment, savoring the camaraderie and the thrill of the game.

With one last look at the emptying field, Dex scooped up his gear and headed for the locker room. The sound of his cleats clicking against the pavement punctuated the end of another day at Sequoia Grove High—a place where victories were more than just numbers on a scoreboard, and where a young man's journey was only just beginning.

The Matthews Residence

Dex's fingers danced over the zippers and buckles of his backpack, each snap and click a step closer to the open sky and whispering pines of Crystal Lake Camp Ground. His room, usually a landscape of scattered football gear and school books, had transformed into an orderly base camp of neatly rolled sleeping bags and stacks of clothes suited for the wilds. The scent of nylon and rubber from his new hiking boots mingled with the familiar comfort of home.

"Seriously, Dex, could you be any louder?" Ava's voice cut through his packing rhythm, her head poking around his bedroom door with a playful scowl etched on her youthful face.

"Shh, Ava, can't you see? I'm practicing my bear scare tactics," Dex quipped without missing a beat, puffing up his chest and letting out a low growl that was more teddy than grizzly.

Ava rolled her eyes, her lips curving into a reluctant grin. "Yeah, because bears are totally scared of oversized puppies."

He chuckled, ruffling her hair in a brotherly fashion. "You just wait, Sis. When we're out there and a big ol' bear shows up, you'll be glad I've perfected my ferocious bark."

"Right, because your barking's gonna send it running for the hills," she teased, ducking under his arm to inspect his packing progress.

Her gaze landed on the assortment of snacks he'd squirreled away—energy bars, trail mix, and a king's ransom of marshmallows. "Planning to feed the entire forest or just us?"

"Us," Dex replied with mock solemnity. "And maybe a squirrel or two. You know how persuasive they can be."

"Especially when they have your eyes," Ava giggled, the sound bubbling through the air like a mountain stream.

"Hey now," Dex said, his tone feigning offense as he swept the last of his gear into the backpack. "Let's keep my dashing good looks out of this."

"Too late, already packed," Ava retorted, zipping up the side pocket where she'd spotted a gap. She paused, glancing up at him with a sudden earnestness. "It's gonna be epic, right?"

"More than epic," Dex assured her, hoisting the pack onto one shoulder to test its weight. It felt solid, reassuring—like his promise. "Adventure is practically calling our names."

"Matthews siblings to the wild!" Ava declared with a flourish, throwing her arms wide as if embracing their upcoming escapade.

"Matthews siblings to the wild," Dex echoed, the corners of his mouth lifting in a smile that reached all the way to his sparkling blue eyes. He slung an arm around Ava's shoulders, guiding her toward the door. "Come on, let's go find some real adventure."

With a shared look of anticipation, they left the organized chaos of Dex's room behind, stepping into the next chapter of memories waiting to be written under the stars.

"Everything's ready to go!" Ava called out, her voice a bright note in the orderly din of preparation.

"Watch your step," Dex cautioned, though his eyes sparkled with mischief. "Wouldn't want the wild to claim us before we even get there."

Ava rolled her eyes but laughed, the sound mixing with the jangle of gear and the soft rustle of leaves in the wind.

Dex's hands were sure and swift as he arranged the supplies in the car, each piece slotted into its perfect place like a puzzle nearing completion. The last item, a battered guitar, was gently nestled in, strings silent for now, poised to bring music to the firelight.

"Let's hit the road!" Dex said, his voice thrumming with the pulse of the journey ahead. He slammed the trunk shut, the sound echoing off the walls of their suburban home—a farewell to the familiar.

"Adventure, here we come!" Ava cheered, mirroring her brother's contagious energy.

"Crystal Lake won't know what hit it," Dex agreed with a laugh that held all the freedom of the skies above them.

And with that, they climbed into the car, seatbelts clicking into place like the final notes of a prelude. Dex's anticipation surged as they pulled away from the curb, his heart beating in rhythm with the turn of the tires, each rotation a step closer to the wildness that awaited at Crystal Lake Camp Ground.

Chapter Five

GHOST STORIES & S'MORES

As the Matthews family car hummed to life, Dex leaned forward between the two front seats, his grin as wide as the horizon. "So, what's the first thing we're doing when we get there?" he asked, his voice tinged with the thrill of impending adventure.

"Unpack, set up camp, and then..." His mother glanced at him through the rearview mirror, her eyes sparkling with shared excitement, "...we conquer that hiking trail we read about. Remember, the one with the breathtaking overlook?"

"Ah, right!" Dex threw his hands up in mock surrender. "How could I forget? You've only mentioned it—what? A hundred times?" He chuckled, dodging the playful swat from his dad.

"Only because it's going to be amazing," his father added, steering the car onto the open road. "And don't forget tonight's campfire. S'mores, ghost stories, and your guitar serenades."

"Can't wait for those s'mores," Ava chimed in, her voice a melody of anticipation.

"Family bonding at its finest," Dex said, winking at Ava. The laughter that followed was warm, wrapping around him like a well-loved blanket.

As miles rolled beneath them, Dex filled the car with tales spun from the threads of his boundless imagination. He recounted the legendary football practice where his fake-out had left spectators gasping, imitating the coach's wide-eyed awe with such precision that his sister snorted with laughter. Dex's story danced, weaving through the cabin, pulling grins from even the most stoic expressions.

"Then," Dex continued, leaning closer to his captive audience, "just as the clock ticked down, I launched the ball. It soared, cut through the air like a comet chasing its tail—"

"Did it make it?" Ava interrupted, her eyes round with suspense.

"Touchdown," Dex exclaimed, punctuating the climax with an emphatic fist pump. "Right in the nick of time!"

The car erupted with cheers, their collective joy a symphony that resonated within the confines of the vehicle. And as the landscape outside whispered by, Dex basked in the glow of shared stories and the soft promise of memories yet to be made, the road unfolding before them like a narrative awaiting its next thrilling chapter.

THE MATTHEWS' family car eased onto the gravel patch, tires crunching a steady rhythm, as Crystal Lake Camp Ground unveiled itself in a panorama of wilderness. The vehicle rolled to a stop, engine quieting, and Dex's gaze swept over the tapestry of greens and blues that painted their home for the weekend.

"Would you look at that view," Dex murmured, his breath fogging the window. Beyond the glass, the lake shimmered, a flawless mirror reflecting the rugged pines reaching skyward around its perimeter.

"Time to make this place ours," Dad announced, popping open the trunk with a click that broke the hush of nature's embrace. "Hey mom," Dad said, trying to get her attention. "We've got company next door."

His mother glanced at the campground adjacent to theirs. Their tents were already up and they had chairs set up around their campfire. "We'll go say hi after we've set up here."

Dex hopped out, stretching limbs still buzzing from the drive and stories shared. He grabbed a tent bag, muscles flexing beneath his worn Sequoia Grove High sweatshirt. The scent of pine needles mingled with the earthy tang of damp soil, filling his lungs and fueling his eagerness. He took a quick glance at the tents already set up next door and didn't give it much thought. "Need a hand with the poles, champ?" he called out to his dad, who was wrestling with the canvas.

"Could use it," Dad grunted, offering a grateful smile as Dex knelt beside him. Together, they unfolded rods that clicked into place, the skeleton of their temporary abode taking shape. Dex's hands moved deftly, experience from past trips guiding him, while his mind danced with the prospect of tonight's campfire tales.

"Hey, Ava," Dex teased, "bet I'll have my tent up before you can finish unpacking your bag."

"Ha, you're on!" Ava retorted, her competitive streak flaring to life as she dashed to her own task.

Dex chuckled, his heart light. The challenge was playful, but his drive to help set the stage for their family's adventure was earnest. With every peg secured and tarp stretched taut, Dex felt a step closer to the evening's camaraderie—a night under stars, where laughter would mingle with the crackle of firewood and the soft whispers of the wilderness.

WITH THE TENTS now standing like proud sentinels amidst the murmuring pines, Dex wiped his brow and shot a grin at Ava. "Race you to the creek?"

"Last one there's a rotten egg!" she squealed, already darting off between the trees.

Dex bolted after her, the ground springy beneath his sneakers. Their laughter tangled with the rustling leaves as they dodged low-hanging branches, the playful competition fueling their speed. He could have outpaced her easily, but he hung back, close enough to ensure she felt the thrill of the chase without stealing her victory.

"Beat ya!" Ava crowed as they skidded to a halt by the babbling brook, her cheeks flushed with triumph.

"Only because I let you," Dex teased, nudging her shoulder gently. She stuck her tongue out at him before turning her attention to the water, captivated by the dance of light over the rippling surface.

"Come on, let's scout for firewood," he suggested, leading the way along the bank where fallen branches littered the ground. The forest seemed to hold its breath, watching as the siblings gathered sticks and logs in a harmonious rhythm.

"Think this will be enough to ward off the ghost of Crystal Lake?" Ava asked, eyes wide as she hoisted a particularly gnarled piece of wood.

"Only if we tell the scariest stories," Dex replied, winking conspiratorially. His heart swelled with a familiar warmth, the shared secret of adventure binding them closer than any campfire tale ever could.

"Race you back?" Ava proposed, her armload of timber making her challenge all the more daring.

"You're on," Dex chuckled, accepting the gauntlet thrown down. As the woods echoed with their footsteps and the promise of an evening filled with stories and starlight loomed ahead, Dex couldn't help but feel that these simple moments were shaping memories that would endure far longer than the flickering flames of their campfire.

.   .   .

DEX HEAVED the last bundle of firewood onto the growing pile, his muscles flexing with the effort. He straightened up, brushing his hands together as he surveyed their collection with a sense of pride. The sun dipped lower in the sky, painting the clouds in hues of orange and purple, signaling the approach of dusk at Crystal Lake Camp Ground. His eyes gleamed with excitement at the thought of the night ahead.

"Tonight's campfire is going to be epic," Dex declared, turning to Ava who was meticulously arranging the smaller twigs into kindling piles. "I've been saving some ghost stories just for this trip."

"Better make them good ones," Ava replied with a playful smirk. "You know Dad's a tough audience."

"Challenge accepted." Dex's voice carried the thrill of anticipation. He imagined the gathering around the fire, the crackle of wood, the flicker of flames casting shadows on their faces as he spun tales that would send shivers down their spines.

"Look at this place, Ava," he murmured, gesturing towards the vast expanse of wilderness that stretched before them. "We're lucky, you know? Not everyone gets to do this."

Ava nodded, her eyes reflecting the same wonderment that Dex felt. The sound of their parents' laughter drifted from where they were setting up the tents, grounding him in the comforting reality of family.

"Super lucky," she agreed. The two siblings shared a smile, a silent acknowledgment of the memories they were creating, woven into the fabric of the mountains and skies of their secluded retreat.

"Let's head back," Dex said after a while, his voice soft but steady. They walked side by side, their footfalls gentle in the blanket of falling dusk. Dex knew that tonight, under the watchful eyes of the constellations, he'd not only be sharing ghost stories but also crafting an unforgettable chapter in the story of their lives.

THE CRACKLE of the campfire punctuated the stillness of the evening as Dex added another log to the flames. Shadows danced across his face, illuminating his sparkling eyes while he settled back into his camping chair. The smell of smoke mingled with pine created an earthy perfume that hung in the night air.

"Alright, everyone, settle in," Dex announced with a grin, rubbing his hands together as if to conjure up the ghost stories from the warmth of the fire. "I've got a tale that'll make you wish for morning."

Ava, curled up in her blanket beside him, shot him a look of mock horror, her eyes wide and playful. Their parents leaned forward, anticipation curling at the corners of their smiles. The scene was set: a family, bound not just by blood but by the shared delight of the moment.

"Once upon a time, right here in these woods," Dex began, his voice dipping low, "there was a—" He paused, his gaze flicking to Ava, who squealed on cue.

"Stop, you're going to scare me!" she protested, half-laughing, half-pleading.

"Scare you?" Dex feigned innocence before winking at her, his tone lightening. "Nah, I'm just setting the mood. But okay, maybe something a little less spooky."

Their parents chuckled, and Dex launched into a different story—one filled with adventure rather than fright, heroes rather than ghosts. As he spoke, his hands gestured with an animator's flair, each movement painting the scene as vividly as the words tumbling from his lips.

Laughter erupted at the punchlines, and even Dex found himself caught in the infectious joy of it all. There was something magical about the campfire glow, the way it seemed to wrap them in its own little world, separate from everything else.

"Remember when Dad caught that fish last year? It was this big!" Dex said, stretching his arms wide. His father scoffed good-naturedly.

"More like this big," he corrected, holding his hands much closer together, eliciting a fresh round of laughter.

"Hey, I have photographic evidence!" Dex retorted, leaning back in triumph as he caught his mother's eye. She shook her head, smiling at the fond memory, the soft lines around her eyes crinkling with amusement.

As the stories continued, weaving a tapestry of past escapades and dreams of future ones, Dex felt a warmth that had nothing to do with the fire. Here, surrounded by his favorite people, the regrets and uncertainties that often hovered at the edges of his thoughts melted away.

He glanced over at Ava, her cheeks rosy from the heat of the flames and her laughter, and realized that moments like these were the threads that held them all together. In the flickering light and the echo of shared joys, Dex discovered a simple truth—these memories were the true adventures of his heart.

The night deepened, stars twinkling overhead like distant campfires, and the family's conversation ebbed into comfortable silence. Dex watched the embers glow, the occasional spark drifting upward, reaching for the sky.

"Thanks, Dex," Ava murmured, her voice carrying a weight of sincerity that tugged at him.

"Anytime, sis," he replied, his voice barely above a whisper, a contented sigh escaping him as he gazed at the fire, feeling the presence of his family like a warm blanket. This was home, he realized—not the walls that housed them, but the love that bound them.

Chapter Six

WE'VE GOT NEIGHBORS

The sun dipped low, casting a golden glow over the Crystal Lake Camp Ground as Maddie's family prepared for dinner. The rustle of leaves in the gentle breeze provided a soundtrack to this yearly ritual.

"Looks like we've got neighbors," her dad announced, nodding towards the adjacent site where another family unfolded chairs and unfurled their own canvas home. Maddie brushed her brown hair from her eyes, securing it with a band she always wore around her wrist for such moments.

"Should we go say hi?" her mom suggested, ever the social butterfly.

"Sure, let's do that," her dad agreed, leading the charge with a friendly wave and a call across the short expanse of grass. "Hello there! Beautiful evening, isn't it?"

Maddie followed, more out of obligation than interest, until her gaze landed on **him**—Dex Matthews. He was tossing a football back and forth with a young girl, probably his sister. His laughter, light and infectious, drifted across the campground, tugging at something deep within her chest. Each throw showcased his athletic grace, each catch a testament to the hours on the junior varsity field.

Her heart performed an unexpected somersault, a silent admission of the crush she harbored, hidden beneath layers of pragmatism. She watched, entranced, as Dex ruffled the girl's hair, his smile reaching his deep blue eyes —the kind of eyes that didn't just look but saw right through you.

"Madison, come meet our new friends!" her mother's voice called, breaking the spell.

Maddie blinked, grounding herself in the reality of introductions and pleasantries. Her feet carried her forward, yet her mind lingered on Dex, his every gesture amplified in significance. *Would she be brave enough to bridge the gap from neighbor to something more? The* thought fluttered in her like a captured bird against the cage of her ribs.

Dex's hand paused mid-toss, the pigskin momentarily forgotten. His gaze, as sharp and clear as the lake waters, shifted from the spiraling ball to the figure of Madison Sullivan standing a short distance away. Something akin to recognition flickered in his eyes, but it was curiosity that truly sparked within their azure depths. He knew her as Brooke Jackson's best friend, a twosome he'd seen in the hallways at school.

Maddie felt the weight of his attention like the sun's rays—warm and unsettling all at once. Her heart, a traitorous drumbeat against her will, urged her forward. She took a deep breath, letting the crisp mountain air fill her lungs, steel her resolve. With each step, her boots crunched over twigs and pebbles, a metronome to her growing determination.

"Hey," she would say, casual, nonchalant. She rehearsed the word in her mind, a single syllable that carried the weight of every unvoiced daydream. As she neared, her shadow mingled with his, a silent dance of light and dark. She could almost hear Brooke's voice in her ear, encouraging, teasing—would have laughed if the flutter in her stomach wasn't threatening to rise up and steal her composure.

Ava's elbow nudged Dex's side, a whisper of conspiracy in her gesture. "Looks like you've got company," she said, nodding toward Maddie with a mischievous twinkle in her bright blue eyes.

"Company?" Dex feigned confusion, but his heart was a drummer boy tapping out an uneven rhythm against his ribs.

"Yep, and she seems to have picked you out of the campground crowd," Ava teased, her voice a gentle chime amidst the rustling of pine needles above.

Dex's gaze flickered back to Maddie, finding her closer now, the distance between them shrinking with each determined step she took. His pulse quickened, a silent drumroll to their impending face-to-face. Maddie's pragmatism seemed to falter for a moment, replaced by a vulnerability that Dex found both endearing and alarming.

"Hey," she said, and it was a wonder how one word could sound like the start of something significant.

"Hey," he mirrored, his voice betraying none of the butterflies performing acrobatics in his stomach. They stood there, awkward soldiers on the battlefield of youthful romance, their glances ricocheting off one another like pebbles skimming across the lake's surface.

The air hummed with the electricity of potential, charged by the golden hues of the setting sun bleeding into the horizon. Dex found himself caught in the orbit of Maddie's hazel eyes—eyes that held stories untold and secrets just beneath their calm exterior.

"Nice night," he managed to say, the words clumsy tools in his usually adept hands.

Maddie nodded, her lips curving into a tentative smile that didn't quite reach her guarded gaze. "It is."

Their conversation was a sapling in the forest of silence, fragile yet reaching toward the light.

Dex shuffled his feet, displacing a few pebbles in the dirt as he searched for words that wouldn't betray the nervous excitement coiling within him. "You go to Sequoia Grove?" he asked, his tone light but revealing an undercurrent of curiosity.

Maddie's response was a smile, her lips parting just enough to let a hint of genuine warmth seep through the practiced composure she wore like armor. "Yeah, it's my sophomore year," she said, her voice steady even as her heart did somersaults behind the fortress of her ribs. "I know you do." *Oh God, oh God, oh God…why did she just say that?!*

Dex grinned, "Do you camp here often?"

Maddie let go an unfamiliar giggle, "Yes, every winter break."

"Same here," Dex replied, his own smile mirrored on his face as if it were common ground they had just discovered.

There was a brief silence—a hesitation before Maddie ventured further into uncharted territory. "Actually, I— I've seen you at lunch a few times," she confessed, the admission slipping out like a secret freed from its cage.

Dex's eyebrows arched slightly, the surprise registering across his features. "Really? I've never seen you around." The words came out more as a reflection of his astonishment than intended doubt.

"Big school," Maddie offered by way of explanation, her hands fidgeting with the hem of her shirt as though seeking something tangible to anchor her in the moment. She could feel the threads of possibility weaving around them, a tapestry still incomplete.

"Guess it is," Dex conceded, his voice carrying a note of wonder. He took in the girl before him anew, as if seeing her for the first time—not just another face in the crowded halls, but someone who shared this slice of the world with him.

Maddie shifted her weight from one foot to the other, a subtle dance of nerves, as she listened to Dex, outline their family's camping itinerary. "We're planning to hike up to the falls tomorrow," he said, his eyes lighting up with the mention of adventure.

"Sounds exciting," Maddie replied, tucking a stray lock of hair behind her ear, her gaze drifting to the towering pines that encircled them like ancient guardians. The late afternoon sun filtered through the branches, casting dappled shadows on the ground and painting the scene in hues of gold and green.

Dex followed her gaze. "Yeah, it's beautiful here, isn't it? Almost like the trees are alive, watching over us."

She nodded, her heart a hummingbird trapped within the cage of her chest. Small talk was a bridge, and she was crossing it with shaky steps, each word a stone laid down carefully. "I love how the lake reflects the sky. It's like two worlds touching," she mused aloud, her voice quieter than she intended.

"Never thought of it that way." Dex's gaze met hers, and there was an echo in his eyes, a silent understanding that made her skin tingle with a mixture of anxiety and anticipation.

"Have you tried canoeing?" Maddie asked, steering the conversation to safer waters, away from the depth she feared.

"Only every winter since I could hold a paddle," Dex chuckled, his grin easy and infectious.

Maddie laughed, a genuine sound that fluttered from her lips before she could catch it. She glanced at him, her hazel eyes meeting his blue ones, and in that instant, she yearned to confess how she'd watched him from afar, drawn to his carefree laughter and sun-kissed hair. But the words lodged in her throat, a silent plea for courage.

"Maybe we could... go together sometime," she ventured, her suggestion hanging in the air like a dragonfly hovering above still water.

"Definitely," he agreed, and there was a lilt in his voice that felt like a promise.

As they continued to talk, Maddie found herself entranced by the rhythm of Dex's speech, the way his hands moved with each description, painting pictures in the air. Her thoughts spun, a carousel of what-ifs and maybes, and she clung to each moment, willing time to slow its relentless march.

Maddie shuffled her feet, her gaze lingering on the rough bark of a nearby pine as if it held answers to the unspoken questions swirling in her mind. Dex, with his effortless charm, seemed to traverse the gap between them without moving an inch.

"Hey, Maddie," he began, a lopsided grin tugging at the corner of his mouth, "do you know why trees are terrible at playing cards?"

Caught off guard, Maddie blinked, her lips parting slightly. She shook her head, curiosity replacing the nervous flutter in her chest.

"Because they always fold," Dex delivered with a theatrical shrug, his eyes crinkling with mirth.

A laugh bubbled up from Maddie's throat, clear and bright as the lake's shimmering surface. It was a simple joke, the kind that might have been lost in the cacophony of a high school hallway, but here, amid the whispering pines, it felt like a lifeline.

"Okay, that was pretty bad," she admitted, but the smile that played on her lips betrayed her amusement. The tension that had thrummed through her moments ago eased, like leaves settling after a gentle breeze.

Dex's chuckle mingled with hers, a harmonious sound that seemed to echo softly against the vast canvas of nature's silence. In this pocket of the world, stripped of distractions and pretense, Maddie found herself adrift in a sea of newfound ease, buoyed by laughter and the quiet hope of connection.

Maddie's fingers twitched toward her jean pocket, the fabric brushing against her skin as she pulled out her phone. Her thumb danced over the screen, eager to spill the day's unexpected turn to Brooke. She imagined the flurry of exclamation points and smiley faces that would crowd the conversation bubble. But as she glanced at the corner of her phone's display, her heart sank—a lone icon taunted her with its emptiness:

`no service`

Chapter Seven

FRISBEE

"Great," she muttered under her breath, the words dissolving into the pine-scented air. The reality of their remote surroundings settled around her like a dense fog, severing the digital lifelines she so often relied on. Maddie cradled the silent device in her palm, the cool glass a stark reminder that here, in this verdant cocoon of wilderness, words had to travel the old-fashioned way—on the wings of her own voice.

Dex's gaze followed the arc of her movements, his eyes narrowing slightly as they locked onto the rectangular object in her hand. "Everything okay?" he asked, his voice threaded with concern. It was soft, like the rustle of leaves underfoot, but it carried across the space between them as surely as if he'd shouted.

"Uh, yeah, just... no cell service," Maddie confessed, feeling the warmth of her cheeks betray her. She tucked the phone back into her pocket, a small surrender to the moment.

"Kinda makes you feel off the grid, huh?" Dex's lips curved into a half-smile, the glint in his blue eyes suggesting he wasn't entirely displeased by the notion.

"Completely," Maddie replied, her laugh a tentative trill that mingled with the distant call of a jay. It was true; the absence of bars on her screen anchored her more firmly to the earth beneath her boots, to the here and now, where anxiety and anticipation swirled together like campfire smoke.

"Maybe it's not such a bad thing," Dex said, shrugging as if to shake off the invisible threads of a world beyond the trees. His casual stance, the ease with which he inhabited the moment, tugged at something within Maddie—a yearning for simplicity, a desire to exist solely in the present.

"Maybe," she echoed, allowing the word to hang between them like a promise yet to be unfolded.

Maddie shoved her phone into the depths of her jean pocket, resigning herself to the silence it represented. "I was just going to text my friend Brooke about all this," she gestured vaguely at the sprawling campground, "but I guess that'll have to wait."

"Brooke Jackson?" Dex's eyebrow arched with a curiosity that felt almost tangible. He knew of Brooke Jackson too. She was the girl all his teammates drooled over. "She your partner-in-crime back at Sequoia Grove?"

"Something like that." Maddie's lips curved into a small, secretive smile, as if the name alone conjured a world of shared whispers and laughter. The pang of disappointment lingered, though, like the last note of a song fading into silence.

Dex followed her gaze to the horizon where the pines stood sentry against the sky, their branches swaying gently in a dance choreographed by the breeze. He turned back to her, his eyes reflecting the afternoon light. "Well, since we're both here and Brooke's not," he said, the corners of his mouth tilting upwards, "we might as well enjoy it, right?"

"Enjoy it?" Maddie echoed, the words coming out more question than agreement.

"Come on," Dex said, a spark of adventure igniting in his gaze. "My sister Ava and I were about to start a game of frisbee before the sun goes down. You should join us."

His invitation hovered between them, a bridge made of hope and maybe a touch of daring.

"Play frisbee?" A flutter of nerves danced in Maddie's stomach. She pictured the disc slicing through the air, the carefree laughter that would surely follow. It was an image so vivid she could almost hear the soft thud of feet on the forest floor, chasing after fleeting shadows and sunlight.

"Yeah, you know, *frisbee*." Dex's voice had taken on a teasing tone. "Round thing, flies pretty well if you've got the knack for it." He mimed a throwing motion, his arm cutting through the air with practiced ease.

"Sure, why not," Maddie found herself saying, the decision sweeping through her like a gust of wind through the leaves. She looked up, meeting Dex's expectant look with a newfound resolve shining in her hazel eyes.

Maddie's feet felt rooted to the forest floor, a tangle of excitement and dread knotting in her chest. She had always navigated her life with careful steps, like threading a needle without a guiding light. The thought of stepping into the unknown, even for something as simple as a game of frisbee, was like peering over the edge of a cliff, the drop-off steep and unforgiving.

"Are you in?" Dex's voice cut through her hesitation, his words a lifeline thrown across the chasm of her doubts.

"I'm... not sure," Maddie admitted, her voice barely louder than the whisper of leaves in the gentle breeze. There was a vulnerability in admitting her uncertainty, like shedding a layer of armor she hadn't known she wore.

"Hey, no pressure," Dex said, his tone light but eyes searching. He seemed to sense the tempest swirling within her, his blue gaze a steady beacon. "It's just a game."

Just a game. The words echoed in Maddie's mind, mingling with the soft rustle of pine needles above them. *But it wasn't just a game, was it?* It was a step closer to Dex, to the heart-fluttering possibility of what might be. Each moment spent with him painted a stroke on the canvas of her guarded heart, the colors vibrant but terrifying in their intensity.

A squirrel scampered nearby, its bushy tail flicking in a dance of carefree abandon. Maddie watched it dart up a tree, envying its unencumbered zest. She took a deep breath, the crisp mountain air filling her lungs, grounding her.

"Okay," she found herself saying, the word a leap of faith. "I'm in."

"Awesome!" Dex's grin was infectious, and for a moment, Maddie allowed herself to be swept up in the ease of his enthusiasm. They walked side by side, the distance between them shrinking with each step. Pebbles crunched underfoot, punctuating their approach to the makeshift frisbee field where Ava waited.

The ground was a patchwork of sun and shadow, and as they crossed into the light, Maddie felt the warmth seep into her skin. With each stride, she shed a layer of her reservations, leaving them behind like fallen leaves. Dex glanced at her, a silent question in his gaze, and Maddie nodded, her smile a silent answer.

"Prepare to be amazed by my epic lack of coordination," she joked, the laughter surprising her as much as it did Dex.

"I'll go easy on you," he promised, winking conspiratorially.

The frisbee soared between them, a bright disk against the expanse of blue above. And as Maddie reached out, her fingertips grazing the spinning edge, the thrill of connection was electric, a current that ran deeper than the game they played. With each toss, each laugh, the threads of a new bond wove tightly around them, stitching together the beginnings of something neither fully understood but both secretly hoped would last.

Chapter Eight

SNOW FLURRIES & AWKWARD GLANCES

The crackling fire cast flickering shadows across Maddie's face as she stole another furtive glance at Dex. He sat mere inches away, close enough that she could smell the woodsmoke clinging to his jacket, yet the distance between them felt vast as the starry sky above.

Maddie's fingers fidgeted with a loose thread on her sleeve. Say something, she urged herself. Anything to break this awkward silence.

"So, um," she began, her voice barely audible over the snapping logs, "what kind of outdoor stuff do you like to do?"

Dex's blue eyes lit up, rivaling the campfire's glow. "Oh man, where to start?" He grinned, running a hand through his tousled blonde hair. "I like to fish, and I'm *huge* into hiking - there's this amazing trail near here with the most insane views. And rock climbing is my absolute jam. Nothing beats the rush of conquering a tough route, you know?"

His enthusiasm was contagious. Maddie found herself smiling despite her nerves. "That sounds pretty incredible," she said. "I've always wanted to try rock climbing, but it seems kind of intimidating."

"Nah, it's not so bad once you get the hang of it," Dex assured her. "I could show you the basics sometime, if you want."

Maddie's heart skipped. *Was he offering to spend time with her, just the two of them? Don't read too much into it,* she cautioned herself. *He's probably just being nice.*

"That would be awesome," she replied, trying to keep her voice steady. "I'd love to learn."

As Dex launched into a story about a particularly harrowing climb, Maddie allowed herself to relax slightly. *Maybe this wouldn't be so awkward after all.* She leaned in, captivated by the way his eyes sparkled as he talked, the campfire's glow warming his features. For a moment, she could almost forget the families surrounding them, lost in their own private world of shared adventure and possibility.

Suddenly, Maddie's parents' voices drifted over, mingling with the deeper tones of Dex's mom and dad. Their laughter punctuated the crackling fire, drawing both sets of adults into an animated conversation about their favorite camping spots.

Maddie's breath caught in her throat. She and Dex were alone – well, as alone as they could be with their families mere feet away. The realization sent her heart into overdrive, thundering against her ribcage like a trapped bird.

What do I say now? Her mind raced, grasping for topics. The flames danced before her eyes, but offered no inspiration. She could feel Dex's presence beside her, solid and warm in the chilly evening air.

"So, um..." Maddie started, her voice trailing off as quickly as it had begun. She mentally kicked herself. *Real smooth, Sullivan.*

Dex turned to her, his blue eyes catching the firelight. A small furrow appeared between his brows as he studied her face. "You okay?" he asked, his tone gentle. "You look like you're solving advanced calculus in your head or something."

Maddie let out a nervous laugh. "Yeah, I'm fine. Just, you know, thinking about... *stuff.*"

Dex's lips quirked into a lopsided grin. He gestured upwards with his chin. "Well, if you're looking for a distraction from all that 'stuff,' check out this snow. I swear, these flakes are so big, we might wake up buried tomorrow. Good thing I brought my snowshoes—we can use them as shovels to dig ourselves out."

Despite herself, Maddie felt a genuine smile spread across her face. The tension in her shoulders eased slightly as she looked up at the gently falling snow. "That's ridiculous," she said, but there was warmth in her voice. "Although, knowing our luck on these trips, we probably should have packed actual shovels."

"Hey, you never know when you might need to dig for buried treasure," Dex quipped, his eyes twinkling with mischief.

Maddie rolled her eyes, but couldn't suppress her grin. "Right, because that happens so often in real life."

As their laughter mingled with the night air, Maddie felt a spark of something unfamiliar yet thrilling. *Maybe, just maybe, this camping trip would be different from all the others.*

Dex's eyes suddenly lit up with mischief. "You know what? I bet I could hit that pine cone over there with a snowball." He pointed to a target about twenty feet away.

Maddie raised an eyebrow, her competitive nature surfacing. "Oh really? I'd like to see you try."

Without hesitation, Dex scooped up a handful of snow, quickly packing it into a ball. He took aim and threw, missing the pine cone by inches.

"Ha! Not as easy as you thought, huh?" Maddie teased, already bending down to form her own snowball.

"Oh, it's on, Sullivan," Dex challenged, his blue eyes sparkling with excitement.

Soon, the air was filled with flying snow and laughter as Maddie and Dex chased each other around the campsite. Maddie's heart raced, but this time from exertion and joy rather than nervousness. She ducked behind a tree, narrowly avoiding one of Dex's well-aimed throws.

"You can't hide forever!" Dex called out, his voice tinged with laughter.

Maddie peeked out, snowball at the ready. "Watch me!"

As they ran and dodged, the awkwardness from earlier

melted away like snow in sunshine. Maddie felt free, caught up in the moment, her usual caution forgotten.

Eventually, breathless and with cheeks flushed from cold and laughter, they made their way back to the campfire. They plopped down on a log, still giggling intermittently.

"Truce?" Dex offered, extending his hand.

Maddie took it, feeling a tiny thrill at the contact. "Truce," she agreed, her voice a little softer than she intended.

As they caught their breath, the crackling fire filled the comfortable silence between them. Maddie found herself stealing glances at Dex, noticing how the firelight danced across his features.

"So," Dex began, breaking the silence, "got any good camping stories? I bet the Sullivans have some wild adventures."

Maddie chuckled, thinking back to past trips. "Well, there was this one time when I was ten..."

Maddie's eyes sparkled as she recounted the memory, her gaze flicking between Dex and the dancing flames. "We were camping here at Crystal Lake, and I decided to go on a solo adventure to find the perfect skipping stone." She paused, a soft smile playing on her lips. "I ended up stumbling upon this hidden cove, with water so clear you could see straight to the bottom."

Dex leaned in, intrigued. "That sounds awesome! Did you find your perfect stone?"

"I did," Maddie nodded, her voice taking on a dreamy quality. "But more than that, I found a place that felt... magical. Like it was just waiting for someone special to share it with." She glanced at Dex meaningfully, her heart fluttering.

But Dex, oblivious to her hint, grinned broadly. "Man, that's cool! We should totally go exploring tomorrow and see if we can find it. I bet Brooke would love to see it too!"

Maddie's smile faltered slightly, but she quickly recovered. "Yeah, maybe," she said, trying to keep the disappointment from her voice.

A gust of wind swept through the campsite, carrying with it a flurry of snowflakes. Maddie shivered, suddenly aware of the dropping temperature. Her brow furrowed as she watched the snow begin to accumulate on the ground.

"Hey, you okay?" Dex asked, noticing her change in demeanor.

Maddie hesitated, then admitted softly, "I'm a little worried about this snow. What if it gets worse? My family's not really prepared for a heavy snowfall."

Dex's expression softened. "I get that. It can be pretty scary when the weather turns unexpectedly." He placed a gentle hand on her shoulder. "But remember, we're all in this together. My family's got some extra gear if you need it, and I'm sure the park rangers are keeping an eye on things."

His words, coupled with the warmth of his touch, brought a small measure of comfort to Maddie. She nodded, grateful for his understanding. "Thanks, Dex. I guess I just needed to hear that."

Snow flurries continued to fall softly around them, Maddie found herself both comforted by Dex's presence and frustrated by his obliviousness to her feelings. She wondered if he'd ever see her as more than just a friend.

The snowflakes danced in the air, their gentle descent creating a mesmerizing curtain of white. Maddie and Dex sat in companionable silence, their eyes fixed on the ethereal scene before them. The crackling fire cast a warm glow on their faces, a stark contrast to the cool, crisp air that nipped at their cheeks.

Maddie's heart raced as she stole a glance at Dex. His profile was illuminated by the flickering flames, his blue eyes reflecting the falling snow. She wondered what he was thinking, if he felt the same electric tension that coursed through her body.

As if sensing her gaze, Dex turned to meet her eyes. For a moment, time seemed to stand still. Maddie felt her breath catch in her throat, the world around them fading away.

Is this it? she thought, her mind whirling with possibilities. *Will he finally see me?*

But before either of them could speak, a voice cut through the night air.

"Maddie! Time to head back, honey!" Her mom's call shattered the moment like glass.

Maddie blinked, reality crashing back. "I... I guess I should go," she stammered, her cheeks flushing with a mix of disappointment and embarrassment.

Dex nodded, a flicker of... something... passing across his face. "Yeah, me too. It's getting pretty late."

They stood, brushing snow from their clothes. As they prepared to part ways, their eyes met once more. Maddie felt her heart skip a beat at the intensity of Dex's gaze.

"Goodnight, Maddie," he said softly, his voice barely above a whisper.

"Goodnight, Dex," she replied, lingering for just a moment longer before reluctantly turning away.

As she walked towards her family's campsite, Maddie's mind raced with conflicting emotions. *What just happened? Was that moment real, or just her imagination running wild?*

Maddie's feet crunched softly on the cold ground as she made her way back to her family's tent. But after a few steps, an irresistible urge seized her. She paused, then slowly turned her head, peering over her shoulder through the gentle cascade of snowflakes.

Dex's figure was retreating into the darkness, his broad shoulders silhouetted against the dim glow of distant campfires. Maddie's heart raced as she watched him go, her mind a whirlwind of emotions.

"What are you doing to me, Dex Matthews?" she whispered to herself, her breath visible in the cold air.

The snow flurries seemed to muffle the world around her, creating a cocoon of silence. In that moment, Maddie felt both exhilarated and terrified. The connection she'd felt with Dex by the fire – *was it real? Or was she reading too much into a simple conversation between friends?*

She hugged herself tightly, partly from the cold and partly from the intensity of her feelings. "Get it together, Maddie," she muttered, trying to shake off the butterflies in her stomach.

But as Dex's form disappeared into the snowy night, Maddie couldn't help but wonder what tomorrow might bring. The Crystal Lake Camp Ground suddenly felt full of possibilities – and potential heartbreak.

With one last look in the direction Dex had gone, Maddie turned back towards her tent, the falling snow seeming to whisper secrets of what was yet to come.

Chapter Nine

The Next Morning

Maddie slipped away from the laughter and clinking of utensils, the voices of her parents and the Matthews melding into a distant hum. With each step toward the shadowed fringe of pines, her boots sank into the cold blanket of snow, a soft crunch marking her passage. Wondering where Dex had vanished, she cast a glance over her shoulder, ensuring no one noticed her departure.

The forest swallowed her whole with its silence. Pine boughs drooped under the weight of winter's touch, casting intricate shadows that danced across the snow as Maddie ventured deeper. Curiosity propelled her forward, her breath forming tiny clouds that dissipated into the chilled air.

"Where could he be?" she murmured to herself, her voice barely above a whisper but loud in the quiet of the woods. Her hazel eyes scanned the landscape, eager for a glimpse of tousled blonde hair or the familiar lines of Dex's easygoing grin.

She moved with purpose, her practical nature guiding her steps even as her heart fluttered with the thrill of seeking out Dex. The snow-laden trees watched in silent witness to her search, their branches creaking like old floorboards under the weight of her secrets.

Her footsteps echoed in the stillness of the winter landscape, a steady rhythm in the vastness of the mountain terrain. Maddie pressed on, determined to find him, her mind painting images of them laughing together by the stream, the one that ran clear and cold even in the heart of December.

The crunch of snow underfoot slowed as Maddie caught sight of him. Dex, perched like a kingfisher on a rock by the stream, his silhouette etched against the fading light, fishing rod in hand. Her pulse quickened—not just from the trek but from the unexpected picture he painted, so absorbed in his task.

Snowflakes began to fall with more intent now, each one a tiny artist rendering the world anew. The air grew thick with them, and the serene tapestry of the forest transformed before her eyes into a canvas of swirling white. Maddie's breath hitched, nature's beauty mingling with an edge of danger.

Maddie shivered and hugged herself close. The cold soaked through her clothes no matter how many layers she wore. The falling snow, which had seemed pretty earlier, now felt scary. It was getting darker and harder to see as the snow fell faster.

A knot formed in her stomach, the previous thrill of finding Dex giving way to concern. *He shouldn't be out here alone,* she thought, the practical side of her mind cataloging the risks. The weather didn't care for teenage whims or secret crushes; it could be unforgiving, even treacherous.

The wind started blowing harder, like it was trying to warn them. She looked back and forth between Dex and the way back to their campsite, not sure if she wanted to stay or get back to safety. The storm was getting worse by the minute, blowing away everything around them and making Maddie feel scared and cold. *They needed to find shelter soon!*

Maddie trudged through the deepening snow, her boots sinking with each determined step. With her heart hammering in her chest, she fixed her gaze on Dex's solitary figure. His blonde hair, flecked with falling snowflakes, contrasted sharply against the evergreens that loomed like silent sentinels around him.

"Dex!" she called out, her voice struggling to rise above the crescendo of the wind that whipped through the trees, snatching away the warmth from her cheeks. He remained a picture of tranquility amidst the chaos, his line disappearing into the icy stream.

"Hey, Maddie!" Dex greeted without looking up, his tone casual, as if they were meeting in the sunlit hallways of Sequoia Grove High rather than in the midst of a burgeoning storm. "What's up?"

She approached, feeling the bite of the cold more acutely with each step. "This weather's getting bad. We should head back," Maddie said, the urgency clear in her voice despite the wind's attempt to swallow her words.

"Ah, it's just a little snow," Dex replied, his eyes still on the water, watching for the telltale tug of a fish. Even though he was acting happy and carefree, Maddie was still really worried. It was like he was trying to be bright and cheerful, but it didn't help her feeling scared at all.

"Seriously, Dex. It's not safe." She wrapped her arms around herself, hoping he would sense the gravity of the situation.

"Come on, Madison," he chuckled, finally glancing up at her with those deep blue eyes that seemed to mock the storm's severity. "Nature's not gonna win this round. Just one good catch, that's all I'm after."

The playful challenge in his voice tugged at her, but Maddie stood firm, her hazel eyes reflecting her resolve. She knew the whimsical dance of snow and wind could turn into a treacherous waltz in an instant. She had to get him to understand, even if it meant pushing past the easy banter that had always been their bridge.

"Please, Dex," she implored, allowing a sliver of vulnerability to seep into her voice, hoping it would be enough to reach him.

Maddie blew out a puff of white air that made a frosty circle around her face. She watched Dex, who looked dark against the thicker snowfall. Snowflakes stuck to his blond hair, and he still had a big smile even though it was getting darker. Maddie's heart pounded fast.

He said nothing, and continued his task.

"Seriously, Dex," Maddie pressed, her voice laced with concern. "It's getting worse out here."

"Just one more fish," he insisted, the stubborn tilt of his jaw cutting through her patience like the icy wind that whipped around them. His eyes were fixed on the liquid ribbon of the stream, his determination as unwavering as the pines that stood sentinel over them.

Despite the warmth that fluttered in her chest at the sight of him so carefree and focused, disappointment crept in, coiling tightly around her resolve. She knew the signs of an oncoming storm; the way the air bit at her cheeks spoke of nature's brewing temper. But there was Dex, casting his line with the hope of victory against the elements.

"Please." The plea hung between them, a fragile thread in the roaring silence of the forest. "We can't risk it."

His chuckle, though light, carried an edge that sliced through her hopes. "Can't let a little snow scare us away, can we? It's just water, Madison. It'll freeze or it'll flow, but either way, I'm not leaving without my prize."

She wanted to argue, to reason with him, but the words dissolved on her tongue, lost to the wind. Maddie realized then that some battles were chosen, and others were conceded. With a heavy heart, she decided this was one she had to walk away from.

"Fine," she said, the single word a white flag in the blizzard of her emotions. "But don't take too long, okay?"

Dex nodded absently, his gaze never leaving the water.

Turning away felt like peeling off a layer of herself, leaving it behind with him. Maddie's practical boots crunched into the freshly laid snow, each step deliberate as she began the solitary trek back to the campsite. The weight of solitude settled upon her shoulders, heavier than the accumulating snowflakes.

The world around her was a canvas of gray and white, the once-familiar path now a blurred impression of what it had been. She trudged on, the chill seeping through her layers, numbing her fingers and nipping at her nose. As the snowfall thickened, so did the mantle of worry for Dex, wrapped around her like a shawl.

Maddie hurried along, leaving the babbling stream talking to itself in the twilight. The thought of a cozy fire and worried faces back at camp made her walk faster. But the further she went, the less sure she felt, like a big question mark in the snowy field.

Her boots crunched deeper into the snow with each step, showing how determined she was. But the woods she knew so well were now a maze of white. The branches were heavy with snow, hiding the path and making it hard to see where she was going.

Oh my gosh, am I lost?!

With every breath, visibility waned, the landscape transforming into a swirling spectacle of flurries. Maddie squinted against the onslaught, her eyelashes catching the delicate snowflakes that dared to venture too close. The world had hushed, save for the muffled crunch of her footsteps and the distant groan of trees swaying under winter's touch.

"Come on, Maddie," she muttered to herself, her voice barely a whisper against the wind's howl. Her head whipped around when she thought she heard her name. *Was that Dex calling out for her?* She turned around, but all she saw was the snow continuing to fall, the trees turning white and the paths closing in.

The landmarks were shy now, revealing themselves only in fleeting glances—a crooked tree here, a boulder capped with snow there—each one an anchor tethering her to the route home. She clung to these glimpses of familiarity like lifelines, her memory painting the trail in broad strokes where her eyes could not see.

A sudden gust whipped through the trees, snatching at her clothes and chilling her to the bone. Maddie shivered, but her steps didn't falter; they couldn't afford to. Every fiber in her body yearned for the warm embrace of the campfire, for the safety of her family's presence.

Almost there, she promised the empty air, her words carrying the weight of a vow. As the snow piled higher, her determination grew roots, anchoring her firmly to her course. Madison Sullivan was no quitter, and this challenge would be met with the same steadfastness that saw her through every trial at Sequoia Grove High.

She moved with purpose, her mind tracing the way back as much as her feet did. Dex's face flickered in her thoughts, a beacon of frustration and concern that spurred her onward. He was out there, somewhere, lost in this same relentless descent of winter.

Please be safe, she thought, the sentiment wrapping around her heart like a scarf. Regret gnawed at her insides, the taste bitter and cold, but this was no time to dwell on what-ifs.

Ahead, a familiar formation of rocks emerged from the whiteness, greeting Maddie like an old friend. A surge of relief washed over her. *This was it, the final stretch.* With renewed vigor, she pressed forward, each step carrying her closer to the warmth of human connection and the hope that Dex, too, would find his way back.

Chapter Ten

QUIET AND WHITE

Maddie's breath formed ghostly puffs in the frigid air, disappearing as quickly as they appeared. Snowflakes clung to her eyelashes, each one a tiny, frozen star melting against her skin. Her boots waded through the accumulating drifts, the sound muffled like whispers in a library.

"Keep moving," she murmured to herself, her voice hoarse from the cold. The words were a mantra, pushing her onward when her body screamed for rest.

It had been more than two hours since Maddie left Dex by the stream, but she still couldn't find her way back to camp. It seemed like the campsite was getting further away every time she took a step.

The snow kept falling, making everything quiet and white. The trees were weighed down by the snow and their branches creaked softly. Maddie was tired from fighting her way through the storm. Her muscles ached and she could barely see.

She started to worry that she might get lost all day. But she wouldn't give up! She thought about her mom's hug and her dad's laugh, and that made her feel braver. Her heart beat fast, like a drum telling her to keep going. She knew her family was strong, and so was she!

Maddie tripped over a root in the snow. She stopped for a moment, leaning against a tree to catch her breath. She looked around at all the white, hoping to see a sign that would help her find her way back.

Then, through the falling snow, Maddie saw something strange. It looked like a building in the distance, almost too good to be true like a dream. *Was it real, or was she just seeing things from being so tired?*

Maddie stood up straight and faced the wind even though it was mad at her for stopping. She knew she should keep going to find camp, but this building seemed like a safe place to rest from the storm. Her legs felt heavy, but she walked towards the mysterious building in the distance, hoping it was real.

Maddie's boots sank into the snow with each labored step, the once-familiar Crystal Lake campground now a treacherous white void. The wind howled, a furious beast intent on pushing her off course.

"Come on, Maddie," she muttered through chattering teeth. "You've got this. Just like the survival guides said."

But those guides hadn't prepared her for **this**. The blizzard intensified, snowflakes stinging her face like tiny needles. Maddie squinted, struggling to see more than a few feet ahead.

I should have listened to Mom about the weather forecast, she thought, regret gnawing at her insides. *Now I might freeze to death because I wanted to prove I could handle myself.*

A particularly strong gust nearly knocked her off her feet. Maddie stumbled, her hands plunging into the icy snow. The cold bit through her gloves, numbing her fingers instantly.

"No," she growled, forcing herself back up. "I won't give up. I can't."

Her legs trembled with exhaustion, each step a monumental effort. The pines that usually comforted her now loomed ominously, their branches weighted with snow, creaking in the wind.

Just as despair threatened to overwhelm her, Maddie's eyes caught a flicker in the distance. *A light?* Her heart raced, hope surging through her veins.

"Please be real," she whispered, blinking furiously to clear her vision.

The light remained, a beacon in the swirling white. Maddie's resolve hardened. She had a goal now, a lifeline to cling to.

With renewed determination, she pressed forward. The wind seemed to fight her every move, as if testing her will to survive. But Maddie was nothing if not stubborn.

"You won't beat me," she said to the storm, her voice barely audible above the howling gale. "I won't quit."

She thought of her family, probably frantic with worry. Of Brooke, her best friend who'd begged her not to go on a hike alone. And inexplicably, of Dexter Matthews, did he make it back to camp?

No, Maddie decided. *I'm not done yet. There are too many things left unsaid, too many adventures still to have.*

Step by agonizing step, she inched closer to the light. It grew stronger, more defined. *A window, perhaps?* Shelter, at last.

Maddie's legs screamed in protest, but she ignored the pain. The light was her only chance, and she'd be damned if she'd let it slip away.

"Almost there," she encouraged herself. "Just a little further."

Maddie's heart leapt as the shadowy outline of a cabin finally emerged from the whiteout. Her relief was so palpable she could taste it, sharp and sweet on her tongue.

"Thank God," she whispered, her voice hoarse and trembling.

As she stumbled the last few feet to the porch, her legs gave out. Maddie caught herself on the railing, her frozen fingers barely able to grip the rough wood. She stood there for a moment, panting, her whole body shaking violently.

"Come on, Maddie," she muttered. "You didn't come this far to freeze on the doorstep."

With a monumental effort, she hauled herself up the creaking steps. The door loomed before her, a barrier between life and death. Maddie reached for the handle, praying it wasn't locked.

The knob turned.

She almost wept with relief as she pushed the door open, practically falling into the dark interior. The wind howled at her back, driving icy fingers of snow into the cabin before she managed to slam the door shut.

A small fire crackled in the fireplace and Maddie instinctively walked towards it for warmth.

Silence fell, broken only by Maddie's ragged breathing.

"Hello?" she called out, her voice echoing in the emptiness.

No answer came.

"Okay," Maddie said to herself, trying to steady her nerves. "You're safe now. Think. *Someone* started the fire. Someone obviously *lives* here."

She surveyed her surroundings. There was a table and two chairs in the corner by a kitchenette. A rug took over most of the wooden floor and some blankets were stacked up in the corner.

Maddie wasn't scared anymore, even though she was still tired. She knew she needed to get warm and dry and see what supplies she had left. As she went inside the dwelling, she started thinking about what to do next, even though a tiny voice inside her worried that this place might be a little creepy being all alone in the storm … but someone started the fire.

Maddie pushed the thought away. She was alive, and that was what mattered. Everything else could wait.

As Maddie's eyes adjusted to the dim light, a sudden movement in the corner startled her. Her heart leaped into her throat.

Dex stepped in through the rear door. Firewood and kindling in his arms.

"Maddie?" He said, dropping the wood next to the hearth. "Thank goodness you're safe … I looked for you."

(To Be Continued …)

PART TWO

Adventure awaits...

Maddie's annual camping trip takes a dramatic turn when a blizzard tears through the mountains, separating her from her family. Seeking refuge in a deserted cabin, she encounters the last person she expects – Dex, the infuriatingly handsome boy from high school and the campsite next door.

Sparks fly in the face of danger...

Forced to rely on each other for survival, Maddie and Dex's

contrasting personalities clash at first. But as the storm rages on, shared stories and flickering candlelight ignite an unexpected warmth between them.

Will their love weather the storm?

With dwindling supplies and no way to contact help, their newfound connection faces its ultimate test. Can their bond survive the harsh reality of their situation, or will it melt away like the snow?

Discover a captivating story of resilience, adventure, and unexpected love.

Part Two!

Young Adult Romance

by Lia Lucas

Ebook & Paperback

About Lia

Lia Lucas is an emerging author of Urban Fiction, Young Adult, and Contemporary Romance. She has a wide range of writing interests and is currently living an incognito digital lifestyle.

Ms. Lucas is part of the Ardent Artist Books family.

Lia has published several books.